This book belongs to:

for Anna and
her children to be

Gran Treavy '06

Waking Day

Landscape at Eragny: church and farm, by Camille Pissarro

a poem by CONSTANCE MORGENSTERN
with fine art by MONET AND FRIENDS

NorthWord
Minnetonka, Minnesota

For so many expressions of Grace

—C. M.

The text and display type were set in ITC Garamond and Zapfino
Composed in the United States of America
Designed by Lois A. Rainwater
Edited by Kristen McCurry

Text © 2006 by Constance Morgenstern
See page 32 for art copyright information
Cover art: *Landscape at Eragny: church and farm,* by Camille Pissarro

Books for Young Readers

11571 K-Tel Drive
Minnetonka, MN 55343
www.tnkidsbooks.com

Library of Congress Cataloging-in-Publication Data

Morgenstern, Constance.
Waking day / by Constance Morgenstern.
p. cm.
ISBN 1-55971-919-2 (hardcover)
1. Impressionism (Art)--Juvenile literature. 2. Light in art--Juvenile
literature. I. Title.

ND1482.I6M67 2006

750'.1'8--dc22

2004030773

Printed in Singapore
10 9 8 7 6 5 4 3 2 1

Light.

Light.

It's quiet as water when it paints the sky.

It flows through the birds like good news,

and builds at your window.

It washes all sleep,

then waits at the door:

Come out, my friend.

Come.

See.

It sets the table with tulips.

It asks the trees to open their hands.

It raises the grass like a magnet.

It makes you feel tall.

It tickles a stream still in bed....

It laughs with the river.

It's curious—

pokes into corners.

It knows the language of cats.

It makes a jacket so fine you hardly know you're wearing it.

It always fits.

It plays hide-and-seek with the clouds,

and slides continually into evening

as if it will never leave the playground.

It stays longer and longer.

It lingers...

until it weaves your fingers with its own,

and shows you the way home.

Morning on the Seine, near Giverny, by Claude Monet

Light.

Morning at Antibes, by Claude Monet

Light.

Ponte Santa Trinita, by Childe Hassam

It's quiet as water when it paints the sky.

Birds Bathing, by Fidelia Bridges

It flows through the birds like good news,

The Studio with Mimosa, by Pierre Bonnard

and builds at your window.

Woman at her Toilet, by Edgar Degas

It washes all sleep,

Outside the Window, by Pierre Bonnard

then waits at the door:
    Come out, my friend.
    Come.
    See.

Early Spring, by Pierre Bonnard

It sets the table with tulips.

Branch of an Almond Tree in Blossom, by Vincent van Gogh

It asks the trees to open their hands.

Orchards in Blossom, View of Arles, by Vincent van Gogh

It raises the grass like a magnet.

Race Horses in front of the Stands, by Edgar Degas

It makes you feel tall.

The Brook, by John Singer Sargent

It tickles a stream still in bed....

Oarsmen at Chatou, by Pierre-Auguste Renoir

It laughs with the river.

Enfants à la Vasque, by Berthe Morisot

It's curious—
pokes into corners.

Chat et Chatte, by Théophile Alexandre Steinlen

It knows the language of cats.

Child in Sunlight, by Frank Weston Benson

It makes a jacket so fine you hardly know you're wearing it.

Alphonsine Fournaise, by Pierre-Auguste Renoir

It always fits.

Big Clouds, by Théo van Rysselberghe

It plays hide-and-seek with the clouds,
and slides continually into evening

The Swing (La balançoire), by Pierre-Auguste Renoir

as if it will never leave the playground.

The Garden Parasol, by Frederick Carl Frieseke

It stays longer and longer.

Five Figures in a Landscape, by Claude Monet

It lingers...

The Sower, by Vincent van Gogh

until it weaves your fingers with its own,

Starry Night over the Rhone River, by Vincent van Gogh

and shows you the way home.

Notes from a Poet

Ah, springtime! It's about light, and colorful new beginnings. I picked the paintings in this book as art for springtime. But did you know there was also a springtime for art?

In the late 1800s, a bright, new style of painting appeared, which was much like a springtime. If you've seen the somber browns and blacks of other famous paintings, you'll know what I mean.

This new style of painting was called impressionism, *and the artworks in this book help tell the story of it, or styles that came out of it. Features of impressionism include rainbow-pure colors, a love of light, and paintings made outdoors. Springtime!*

The French artist **Claude Monet** (who lived from 1840 to 1926) helped start impressionism, just as he starts this book.

Monet painted *Morning on the Seine* at sunrise, from a special boat he used for painting. (Can you tell?) Pretend you are with him there, in the early sun and fog. Monet paints to capture the delicate colors in the water, sky, and trees. Yet, the sun keeps rising, and the colors in the fog quickly change. Monet puts aside his half-finished painting, then chooses another. A reporter (who really did ride in the boat) wrote that Monet had 14 paintings of the same scene! But each one, to Monet, had a different light.

You'll see Monet's love of light in all three of his paintings in this book. In *Five Figures in a Landscape,* you'll also see five of his eight children and stepchildren.

The French artist **Camille Pissarro** (1830-1903), whose work is on our cover, was another leader of impressionism. Other artists called him "Father Pissarro," but not just because his five sons went on to be artists. "Father Pissarro" earned his name by encouraging so many impressionist painters.

And the impressionists needed encouragement! At that time in France, there was an official art show, which often refused to include their works. The judges of the show preferred artworks of important, historical subjects that were carefully painted in studios. Instead, the impressionists went out to paint the light and the everyday life that they saw, in a style that was a bit like "coloring outside the lines."

When these artists opened their own art show, even the public had doubts, because their paintings were so different. A magazine writer called their style "impressionism" as a putdown! But I think there is a spring-like freedom to their work, and a good measure of joy.

Pierre-Auguste Renoir (1841-1919), in particular, liked to paint happy things. Do you feel it? He tried to make paintings that he himself would want to "walk into." When I was growing up, his was the first art I wanted for my wall.

Edgar Degas (1834-1917) helped start the impressionists' art shows, and he displayed his work in most of them. Still, he didn't like to be called an "impressionist," and he preferred to paint indoors. One of his favorite subjects was ballet dancers.

Berthe Morisot (1841-1895) was a respected woman painter, which was unusual. (For one thing, women could not yet attend the public painting school.) Morisot, however, learned her craft through private lessons.

Enfants à la Vasque shows her daughter, Julie Manet, at play over a water basin.

While impressionism started largely in France—you'll hear these painters called "the French impressionists"—the style did spread. Three Americans who came to France to learn from the impressionists were Frederick Frieseke, Frank Weston Benson, and Childe Hassam.

Frederick Carl Frieseke (1874-1939) loved the work of Renoir, though he became a neighbor of Monet when he moved to France. *The Garden Parasol* shows his wife, Sarah, in their yard near Monet's.

Frank Weston Benson (1862-1951) received a ticket to Paris, France, for his twenty-first birthday. Some of his most popular paintings depict his wife or daughters on an island of Maine.

Childe Hassam (1859-1935) also studied in Europe and even lived in an apartment once occupied by Renoir.

He painted *Ponte Santa Trinita* while on an art trip to Florence, Italy.

Impressionism had gained respect, so that many artists of that time began to use features of it. Yet, not all of the artists in this book were considered, in general, to be impressionists.

John Singer Sargent (1856-1925), who was an American living in Europe, earned his reputation for painting portraits of people.

Fidelia Bridges (1834-1923), an American woman, painted birds and flowers—but usually with too much detail to be called an impressionist.

Théophile Alexandre Steinlen (1859-1923), who was born in Switzerland, is especially remembered for posters. Because his later home in Paris had so many cats, it was called "the cat cottage."

When I see a poster of cats, I check its label for "Steinlen," the same way I check a painting of ballet dancers for "Degas." Often, however, the style of an artist's work gives as big a clue as the subject.

If you look closely at *Big Clouds* by Belgian artist **Théo van Rysselberghe** (1862-1926), you'll see that the work is made of many spots of paint. This style, called "pointillism," is one that came out of impressionism. Just as the impressionists had changed the rules of earlier painting, other painters changed the rules again.

Dutch painter **Vincent van Gogh** (1853-1890) was one of these. You can see that he adopted ideas of impressionism (and even pointillism) in his paintings, but for him it wasn't enough to try to paint what he saw, without adding extra meaning through color.

Van Gogh struggled with strong emotions all his life (he cut off his own ear after a violent argument with painter Paul Gauguin). He also sold only one painting at a good price during his lifetime. It was his brother Theo who provided friendship and art supplies. When Theo had a baby son, van Gogh worked hard to paint *Branch of an Almond Tree in Blossom,* as a gift.

Frenchman **Pierre Bonnard** (1867-1947) admired both van Gogh and Monet. He agreed with van Gogh, however, that painters should choose their colors to help express emotion. Bonnard wrote in his diary that "cutting out a piece of nature and copying it" is "untruth."

Yet, Monet's words of advice to another painter sound exactly like copying nature! He says to "forget what objects you have before you, a tree, a house, a field, or whatever. Merely think, here is a little square of blue, here an oblong of pink, here a streak of yellow, and paint it just as it looks to you...."

Yes, art ideas change like the seasons! But, for me, impressionism will always be the springtime.

photo by James Morgenstern

CONSTANCE MORGENSTERN likes to paint with words.
She is a published poet and the author of four children's books.
A former teacher, she also has given poetry workshops to
elementary and middle-school students. Ms. Morgenstern lives in Wisconsin.